INTO THE WILDS

INTO
THE WILDS

fw

Copyright © individual authors 2022

First published in 2022 by
Fox & Windmill Books

www.foxandwindmill.co.uk

British Library Cataloguing-in-Publication data
A catalogue record for this book is available from the British Library

Paperback 978-1-8384863-0-3

Printed and bound in the UK by Short Run Press

Reviews

An immersive collection of wry, absorbing, surprising stories about the human condition. Lust, loss, grief and jealousy mix with themes of family, responsibility and identity, proving that there's no such thing as the singular South-Asian experience – *Kia Abdullah*

A great collection of work from some of your favourite writers right now and the stars of tomorrow, from an important imprint finding the best South Asian writers out there – *Nikesh Shukla*

A brilliant collection of writers and writing from Fox and Windmill; it's great to find new work from writers of all ages celebrating and questioning what it means to be alive in the world and pay attention to the things which others might miss – *Andrew McMillian*

This anthology is a timely, vital publication which clearly demonstrates the wide-ranging talent from the British South Asian community. The short-stories and poems are relatable, at times haunting and certainly written by writers who have bright careers ahead of them – *Amit Dhand*

Acknowledgements

First and foremost we'd like to thank our mentor, Kevin Duffy, who advised, encouraged and inspired us every day.

We'd like to thank our families for their continued support, enthusiasm and love when we began F&W and for giving us the courage to chase our dreams when they had to give up theirs.

Habiba & Sara

Introduction

Books were my first love. I loved the way they smelt, the way they felt in my hand, and the promise of what they held. I loved books so much that my first small act of rebellion was sneaking off to a bookshop in the centre of town. Granted, I wasn't much of a rebel but to a young girl growing up in the heart of inner-city Bradford, books were my escape.

The books I bought during my childhood came from WHSmith. The beautiful Waterstones that is housed in The Wool Exchange didn't open until I was 22. So, I read stories like *Little Women*, *Anne of Green Gables* and *Wuthering Heights*. Whilst I loved them, the characters' lives were far removed from mine. I had a vivid imagination, and these books gave me an insight into the kind of lives I'd never live. But it meant that as a child, when I began writing, I didn't feel allowed to write about brown, Muslim girls in the North of England.

Without realising it, I had internalised my place in the world in relation to white people. The teachers at the Catholic Girl's School were white, they had little knowledge of my home life, and what they knew was based on assumption. I learnt to minimise myself and it took years for that damage to be undone. As a teenager, the only place I could find books by people of colour was in a small shop behind the city's Arndale Mall. *Shared Earth* was situated on a hill and was filled with dreamcatchers, tarot cards and tie-dyed clothes. The scent of incense hit you as soon as you walked in through the beaded doorway. At the back of the shop, there was a bookcase filled with books from across the world. There was a diverse mix of memoir, political speeches, and books about activism. While there weren't books about British Asian women there, I did discover books about people of colour. I found Maya Angelou and Malcolm X. I was hungry to see myself reflected in the pages of a book, I wanted to see what was possible for people like me.

In order to fulfil our dreams and reach our potential, we need to see people who look like us doing the things we aspire to. We need to hear names that sound like ours in the pages of a book and in positions of power, because before we can become something, we need to believe it can exist. The achievement begins long before the practice, the test, the win. It begins in the mind when we form the idea of what we want to be and who we will be.

That is why this book and Fox & Windmill are so important. Habiba and Sara are doing world-changing work. They are planting the seeds of possibility, one that generations to come will reap the benefits of. It will allow people of different backgrounds to access our experiences in a way that does not traumatise us. If playing fields are to be balanced, we need to be able to access to each other's stories. Equally, the speed at which information is disseminated means the world is getting smaller and as industry centres move into Asia, it is beneficial for anyone wanting a seat at the table, to build understanding of the diaspora communities that live in the UK and to learn from them. The intersectionality of being South Asian and Northern carries with it a double whammy of stigma. The Northern British Asian experience is very different from the Scottish Asian experience, and from the British Asian experience of those raised in London.

Being the child of two worlds comes with complications and joys. The cities that our parents made their homes and where we're raised, add nuance to our character and experience.

The rich landscape of the hills and valleys of Yorkshire has fed and watered our souls. The life cycle of Bradford's mills, the rise and fall of the textile industry, the birthing of artists and writers, these are all part of our collective heritage. A heritage that is fertile ground for storytellers.

Stories allow us to talk about our experiences in safety and give us a space to explain ourselves if we choose to, or indeed if we become tired of explaining, we hold our tongues. Words are powerful, they bring change at a cellular level. The characters that we create become friends and enemies to our readers, inspiring loyalty and understanding. In the absence of role models, they show us what is possible.

When I decided I wanted to be a writer, I had no idea how publishing worked. *The Writers and Artists Workbook* was a friend, then I found Twitter, and connected with other writers, agents, publishers and editors. My entire career from journalism to a novelist, has been one of trial and error. There were times when it felt as if I was fumbling around in the dark, falling and getting back up to try again. As a published writer and a successful journalist, I see now that it doesn't have to be this way. As the child of an immigrant, I lacked a network and as pre-internet teen, information was harder to come by.

Things are different now, but there is still a long way to go. Hopefully Fox & Windmill will push things along even further, encouraging people who have stories within them to believe it is possible to become published writers. I look forward to watching Habiba and Sara push the boundaries of publishing, and step into their power.

Saima Mir

Prayer

Zaffar Kunial

First heard words, delivered to this right ear
Allah hu Akbar – God is great – by my father
in the Queen Elizabeth maternity ward.
God's breath in man returning to his birth,
says Herbert, is prayer. If I continued

his lines from there, from *birth* – a break Herbert
chimes with *heav'n and earth* – I'd keep in thought
my mum on a Hereford hospital bed
and say what prayer couldn't end. I'd say
I made an animal noise, hurled language's hurt

at midday, when word had come. Cancer. Now so spread
by midnight her rings were off.
                                                    I stayed on. At her bed.
Earlier, time and rhythm flatlining, I whispered
Thank you   I love you   thank you
        mouth at her ear.
She stared on, ahead. I won't know if she heard.

Agraha

Amaleena Damlé

eat more! have more! a prelude to
silver trays that glint like luminous
sparklers against the ebony of antique wood
straight-backed barley-twist chairs sudden
thrones for a suburban Diwali feast.

eat more! have more! a ringing refrain
to clatter over plates piled high
silken sweets fecund with milk and fruit
the pastry shells of crescent moons
spilling their syrupy coconut flesh.

eat more! have more! the chant of a mother's
labour infused in crisp salt-laced spirals
encrusted in flakes of puffed rice and nuts
you lift with a spoon, cradle in your hand
and catapult to scratch the back of your throat.

eat more! have more! the tenderest of exhortations
an overture to see your face reflected in deities
share in their celestial *prasad*, fill yourself up with
duty and devotion, each morsel patterning your
insides with the supplications of chilli and mace.

3

Just the Three of Us

Sangeeta Mulay

"LIGHTS! CAMERA! ACTION!" the director bellowed.

The extravagant set, erected in the hope of getting Rs.100 crore returns at the box office, shuddered into action. The middle-aged, surgically chiselled body of my Bollywood hero glistened. His transplanted hair shone. The steroid induced muscles made his arms look like two pumped-up, brown balloons. Ron Kumar radiated an aura unique to the successful few of Bollywood. His short and easy to pronounce screen name, chosen so as to not grate on the tongues of the audience, had guaranteed box-office returns for the past twenty-five years. He sat smoking, owning the space, his legs spread out and shirt unbuttoned while his body double performed a dangerous fight sequence, taking a kick from the villain in his stomach, performing two somersaults in quick succession and finishing off with a neat martial art kick.

It was my first Bollywood movie. A love triangle – two damsels in love and awe with one dashing hero.

"We'll create something unique," the director claimed, "never before witnessed in the history of Bollywood." We set forth with the best of intentions. This was the industry's seven-hundredth love triangle, but hope ruled. We had a male superstar on board, after all.

After a short wait, it was my turn. My first love scene with my hero. Adorned in a twenty kilograms *ghagra* with heavy ornaments, my lungs felt compressed. My hero wore a casual, white shirt. An air conditioner had been brought on to the set to prevent the moistening of our armpits. A make-up man was nearby to slather our faces with chemicals when needed. Our individual stylists neatly arranged our curls and locks to specific requirements whenever they got the chance. As I looked with lustful eyes at Ron Kumar, the third angle of the triangle, Mina, looking like a Mughal work of art in a guava-coloured sari, watched from the shadows.

Ron Kumar and Mina. The hit Bollywood pair who never failed to delight the audience. He was known for his swag, and she for her dance moves. He was known to carry films on his shoulders while she provided the glamour quotient. He, the perfect lover while she, the pure goddess and hot girlfriend all rolled into one — a complete, tantalising package of allure and goodness. And then there was me — the newbie, the salt in their *gulab jamun*, a chilli in their cake, sugar in their Biryani.

"I want to see lust in your eyes, Sara," hollered the director as he pranced around, "Show me that you desire him. It's all in the eyes."

An attempt was made to summon lust. Ron Kumar held me by my waist. My left arm on his right shoulder. I looked into his eyes and spotted a tiny bogey in his left eye. My lips quivered. Eyelids fluttered. Muscles ached. I wanted to scratch my calf and get into something comfortable — to stetch and yawn. Instead, I gazed coy and adoring at my hero as if he was my one and only. His breath made me think of bits of egg rotting in the crevices of his teeth. I tried to pour the sentiments of *'I'm nothing without you'* in my gaze. His exposed chest was the colour of tandoori chicken. Rescue me, my alpha man — my body attempted to scream. Throughout, my hero made sounds like a constipated individual finding the ultimate release. My eyes failed to reveal my exasperation. I was a good actor, after all. I turned to look at Mina. Her eyes, like a poignant ghazal, met mine and spoke to me from the side-lines. I moved a facial muscle to hint at warmth and happiness. Words were unnecessary.

Ron Kumar held me. His hand lightly brushed my chest as if doing me a favour. Lust miraculously showed in my eyes and for a few seconds, the actor in me rejoiced. Ron Kumar got the validation he needed, and his eyes reflected his victory for a second. It's strange, but real life gets lived in these fleeting seconds. Everything else is just show and artifice.

But I'd rejoiced too soon.

"And CUT!" the director shouted, "Lust Sara. Lust. It's missing."

Ron Kumar walked with a casual confidence back to his chair in the manner of a man used to the silliness of nervous girls.

"Let's take a break," the director said, "We'll try again tomorrow."

I turned to Mina. Our eyes sealed a deal. She came home with me. That evening, we laughed together, sharing stories of compromises. The evening was enjoyable. I wished to mark it with something special. Skipping to my room, I dug out the precious box and ensconced it in a wrapper that hinted luxury.

"For you," I said to Mina.

"A gift?" she asked. Her eyes looked happy like a myna bird singing in spring.

"Open it," I said.

She unwrapped the gift and gently opened the pink and gold box to reveal a necklace. The size of the sparkling stone made her blaspheme. I laughed.

"It's artificial," I said.

"But it sparkles!" she said.

"Wear it," I urged. So, she did. The evening was deposited as a special one.

Summoning lust was easy the next day. My lips quivered. Eyelids fluttered. I'm nothing without you. I desire you. Take me in your arms.

Protect me. Save me from this cruel, unfair world. Oh, my hero. Ravish me! My body, my eyes, my soul; my entire self, screamed out at Ron Kumar in a helpless damsel kind of a way. My eyes were on my hero, but I looked at Mina. The light caught the sparkly stone in her necklace and the pretty rainbow effect reminded me of the kiss we'd shared last night. I knew I'd delivered a perfect shot. That's all it takes. I thought to myself.

"And CUT!" the director's shriek brought me out of my reverie. "Excellent!" the director beamed, "And PACK UP." He turned to Ron Kumar and winked. "Your sex appeal never fails," he smirked, unconcerned about me.

My Bollywood hero gloated. He held me for just a minute longer than was necessary. Walking with a swagger, he returned to his make-up van.

The Season of Pomegranates

Mariam Tasneem Chaudhry

Meet me by the pomegranate tree, she would say
that fruit of the heavens
when your morning work is done
pack up your things and come to me
and I shall wait for you
I shall wait for you to join me.

And I would run
against the direction of the brook
which flowed alongside
above and below
rocks and pebbles.
It would lead me to her

And it would remind me of the life in her laughter
I was hungry for her laughter
and she would sit there
in the same spot
the branches of the pomegranate tree
bowing above and around her.
The large ripe fruit hanging like
striking red lanterns

Heavy and full and sweet.
Her Khamak embroidered shawl
gracefully balanced upon her head
and shoulders.
And I would pause, breathless
taking it in, taking *her* in
and then she would see me
and she would smile
and she would fill me up.

A White Boy Is Looking At You

Sarah M Jasat

You check behind you. Is he looking past you? No, you are in the first row of the near-empty lecture theatre. There is nothing ahead of you except your professor, fiddling with the projector to bring the graphs on her slides in and out of focus. The seats around you are empty, save for your backpack full of files and library books.

You push the hair that has fallen loose from your plait back behind your ear and fidget with your pen. You pretend to search for something in your backpack, so you can peek behind you again. Perhaps you were mistaken. You sneak a glance over your shoulder. The white boy is still looking at you.

He is handsome. You have seen him before. You have taken inventory of his messy brown hair, his strong jaw and his bobbing Adam's apple. Noted his long fingers with short nails, his deep voice. You have filed these details away as irrelevant.

Filing aside, you would, if presented with the option, *swipe right*. But you would never be presented with the option, would you? Growing up as the only Indian in your primary school and one of five in the local secondary, white boys have somehow always known you were not on the menu, not a real girl of flesh and blood. Their eyes slid straight over your dark dull features and your scrawny figure swathed in clothes picked out by your mother. You've made improvements since then, you remind yourself. Your eyebrows no longer merge with your hairline, and your upper lip is fortnightly threaded by rolling appointments at Bab's Beauty. You pick your own clothes now, have breasts and hips though you don't wield them with any finesse. You like the way you look. You like yourself. You toss your plait over your shoulder and sit up straight. This isn't school, where little children might reject the unfamiliar. Why shouldn't the white boy be looking at you?

You take your time packing away after class, sliding your pens and pencils into your case, organising your backpack and giving him time to pack his own things. To muster his nerve and approach you. You hear his footsteps on the stairs as he thuds down to the front row. You keep your back to him, zipping your bag up with more care than you have ever taken in your life. You hear him clear his throat. He says your name and you turn, stunned. A further miracle: his pronunciation is almost correct. Did he hear the professor when you raised your hand for the first question of the lecture today? Or, perhaps, did he notice you long ago? Has he been looking at you all this time, and you simply haven't realised until now?

He is talking to you. You are walking with him. The two of you are a pair. You reach the door and he opens it for you, just like in the films. A group of girls walk past and you feel their gaze, feel them wonder what you have done to attract his attention. There are not too many other girls in this class, but there are some. Girls with manes of brown or blonde hair, who look runway ready in their varsity tracksuits and Ugg boots. They wear chunky knit scarves and hold drinks from the on-campus Starbucks as they wait outside lecture halls, chatting and laughing. These are the kinds of girls that everyone expects the white boy to look at.

What have your cousins said? That you should have more confidence. That you should try to make something of yourself. Surely there are plenty of boys who would be interested.

Of course, they mean brown boys who might dare to message you a few times and take you on covert dates to Nandos, but will sooner or later bring their parents to your house. They would never have meant this white boy, but that's their mistake, isn't it? They underestimated you.

I see you, he seems to be saying, although the words don't quite sync with his mouth. You've made it.

You belong. You're welcome here, which is everywhere. He gestures with his hand and you follow the movement, seeing opportunities spark in its wake. Dates in restaurants with tablecloths, art galleries and the theatre, introducing him to your cousins and seeing their expressions sick with jealousy. 'Yes,' you'll say casually, 'you were right. There were boys interested after all.'

Your parents will be difficult, you know, but eventually even they will be swayed by his confident manner of talking, the smart way he holds himself and the life he can offer you. He has chosen you and who are they in their two-bed terrace, with the lingering smell of fried onions, to stand in your way? And if their small minds cannot comprehend your new life, little pity. You can shrug off your old family ties and the heavy responsibilities that come with them. You're headed for a new path now.

The white boy has stopped talking. He is waiting for some answer from you. You heard only the shape and sparkle of his smile. You ask, with a self-conscious laugh, if he can repeat himself. You listen carefully to the words this time, not wanting to shatter his good opinion of you, keen to show that he was right in choosing you.

The white boy wants to know how you are getting on with the data plotting coursework that is worth thirty-five percent of your end of year grade. The white boy has been finding it difficult. The white boy was wondering if the two of you could meet up and work on it together. The white boy wonders if you could give him some pointers, since you seem to understand the lecture material so well.

You look at the white boy. You understand now that he was not looking at you at all. He was looking at a tool he requires. He had not seen you, but a spare pen when his ran out, or the free shuttle bus when he's running late. A way for him to get what he needs and nothing more. He is waiting for you to answer, expecting that he already knows what you will say, because it will be what everyone says. It is what you would have said if you had even the slightest suggestion that his aim was anything more than a higher mark on an important piece of coursework, a first-class degree and the comfortable job it will afford him.

"I'm free now," he says. "We could stop by the library."

You have paused for too long and the easy atmosphere between the two of you has dropped away. He is trying to help you, trying to facilitate the agreement he knows you were about to give.

"I'm sorry," you say. "I've got to get home."

You eat dinner while on a video call with your family and spend that night, and the nights and weeks after, plotting data set after data set into Microsoft Excel. You explore different algorithms, creating graphs and dissecting their strengths and shortcomings in excessive detail, until you have exceeded the word count for the assignment several times over. You spend another week cutting it back down so it can be accepted by the online submission portal.

You are not surprised when you achieve a first. At the end of term, your professor calls you to the front to comment on the elegant way you referenced her latest publication in your assignment. You think you see the white boy looking in your direction, but when you turn to walk back to your seat, he is looking at the girl sitting next to him, playing with her hand and making her giggle.

He doesn't look at you again. Not for the rest of the year. Not even at graduation when you walk across the stage to receive the award for the highest grade in your cohort, while your parents holler and clap from the front row.

That white boy looked at you only once, but he never saw you. As you grasp your diploma and smile for the award photo, you're glad of it.

Morning Walk around Boudha Stupa

Sujana Crawford

I wade through a sea of red robes,
bathe in its chants. It reminds me
how local women gathered around

a communal *dhunge dhara* here once.
A few metres away bustles another world.
Young mothers spread *lapsi, khapse*

and bowls of *makai* under Buddha's
all-seeing eyes. *Feed the pigeons*, they coax,
they'll carry away your strife.

I bite my tongue at the price,
watch pigeons take flight at their
sudden collective chortle.

My hands no longer reach for the
prayer wheels, they ignore the butter lamps.
Through an open window, I spy a woman

steady the day ahead,
her family, like the morning sun,
still warm under thick cotton *odhane.*

The *gallis* that raised me barely recognise
me anymore. I pretend not to care,
look the other way

just as a group of young monks
drift away in a wave of red robes.
I have nothing else to wish for.

The Guesthouse

Majida Begum

Sofia slowly made space. She found homes for Adam's favourite ties and cufflinks, she filled beautiful wooden boxes with almost empty perfume bottles, a comb, his notebooks and diaries over the years. They were tucked away under the bed or in the bottom shelf of her wardrobe.

There were other things she displayed in the house with pride. His tasbeeh sat on her bedside table, his treasured copy of Machiavelli's *The Prince* sat alongside the hardback vintage copy of *Jane Eyre* he had gifted her all those years ago. The Qur'an which he read daily, occupied the same shelf as her Qur'an.

These pieces became her anchors in the house. She would pass by them and sigh, read a few ayahs... 'Indeed, we belong to Allah, and indeed to Him we will return' and continue with her day.

They were dotted around the house in such a way that his presence never left their home. There were some nights that she would stay up to read the annotations he left behind in the margins of books he had read. Sofia had traced every word he wrote and the crooked underlining of every sentence that had resonated with him in some way. The ink had started to smudge, some of the pages now felt old and crinkled. She would remember a thought he once shared and it became more poignant too, it would become her mantra that week and carry her through. It was as though she was falling in love with him all over again, remembering him and observing him all over again, only now, with an impermeable distance.

She soaked in the warmth of this familiarity and continued to make his favourite dishes. They became the meals she looked forward to the most, she seemed to discover a part of herself, all over again, through this familiarity. In her grief, she moved closer to him. There was a fullness in all of this, a return of sorts.

The uncle who served her at the butchers never questioned her routine, the uncle at the Sunnah shop packaged the same items for her, he never showed her the new products or offered a discount on the last pieces. Her bedding remained the same too, she kept an extra pillow where Adam slept, just as he had liked it.

Her friends, Maryam and Ava never questioned the extra laundry or why the home always smelt the same. Sofia's comfort became theirs. They left cups of chamomile and lavender tea by her side silently on the nights she stayed up re-reading Adam's books. They placed blankets nearby and a cushion for her back and closed the windows. They made sure to pray Fajr together on those nights. They stopped worrying; they knew that in the morning there would be a cup of tea to be had, a breath to take and the day would begin all over again.

Sofia would have understood her grief further; her sigh would be lighter that day and her tea sweeter. They didn't mention it in the morning. They did not rub their eyes or have extra coffee before work and Sofia didn't ask why Maryam had stayed over that night. It was a silent solidarity amongst them all, an extra tight hug as they left for work that morning.

Ava had long begun to feel at ease with the cycles of grief, she could even notice the beauty in it. In the first few months following her own divorce, Sofia never left her side. Maryam would arrive at their catch ups with a plant for Ava: a small devils ivy, a string of hearts, a calathea. Ava accepted the plants, never expressing her concern about taking care of the delicate life forms alongside taking care of her daughter. She didn't realise how Maryam had shifted her attention and care that had felt lost in the break up to giving the devils ivy enough sun, untangling the string of hearts and dusting the leaves of the calathea.

Most of that time felt hazy to Ava now, but she remembered how Sofia had been her anchor. Sofia had taken Ava and her young daughter in, as if they were her own. She had grieved the loss of Ava's marriage with her and now, Ava had grown to appreciate the cycles of grief and her role within it. She grew fond of the scents in Sofia and Adam's home that had now become her home too. She was proud of Sofia and how she continued to make space despite being tested with such loss. She watched with admiration as Sofia slowly emptied cupboards that would now be filled with her daughter's shoes and bags, Maryam's loose-leaf teas and Ava's tea sets.

Now, Maryam brought in plants every time she came to stay at Sofia's for a few nights. Lemon trees thrived across the tiled dining and kitchen area and spider plants grew rapidly in each bathroom. Sofia integrated watering the plants into her routine. She would stop and ponder how the leaves had grown today and how much brighter that lemon looked... it would prompt her to clutch onto her clothing and feel for the kick of her baby that was growing in her stomach. These moments became anchors in her routine.

The girls had no idea all those years ago at *The Guesthouse,* their favourite café, that they would be here. Ava and Sofia – living together with Ava's daughter and Sofia, expecting a baby she never imagined, without Adam here. And Maryam, a wandering writer, still figuring it all out, married to the man she had imagined existing and hoped existed for her.

In *The Guesthouse*, they chatted for hours, over endless cups of peppermint tea, chai lattes and coconut flat whites. In those few hours, they had bonded over summer flings and their complicated relationships with their parents. It had been the summer of graduation for Maryam, the summer before she started her grown up job. She had said a rather rushed goodbye to Cambridge, to the city that gave her so much space and much needed air. A dream-like space in the form of long walks to lectures, past a scurry of cyclists and oat-milk stocked cafes, amidst the nightmarish weekly essays.

Maryam had returned to East London after three years away to resume her life, only as a completely different person. To fit neatly into a space that seemed rather illusive now and seemed not to exist.

She became the big sister and the daughter again, the weight of duty, obligation, and responsibility returned. Her developing friendship with her childhood best friends, Ava and Sofia, felt like a lifeline of sorts – in it she was allowed, once again, to have a mosaic of an existence; one that was varied and filled with conversations about their experiences, dreams and hopes. With them, her life was still large, she was still full of life. They brought a newness that was hopeful, warm, and full of the comfort that she needed.

In the beginning it was Ava that Maryam was most drawn to. Ava had exuded confidence that afternoon, she casually spoke about her dreams, as though it was already written and already within reach. God, she wore confidence so well. She still did. It was one of the things Maryam loved so much about Ava.

That long summer afternoon, Ava had mentioned her cheating boyfriend almost like a passing moment, as though it had barely touched her. She sounded free as she said it; there was no sense of loss. There was an aura of clarity and confidence accompanying her retelling of events.

In another life, Ava would have been a performer – a lead singer or dancer even. Ava's clarity became a lens for Maryam to look through as she thought about her life and the worries she carried with her. Ava had so swiftly, graciously and with ease packed away the heartbreak she had endured. She had quite simply turned the page.

Maryam had wished at that moment that she could package that and carry it with her. It was Ava's presence that carried her in those first few months of their friendship. Her hopes and dreams included Maryam, they seemed big enough and to have welcomed her with both hands.

As she continued the somewhat mundane and repetitive motions of her life now, walking to her office by East Village, stopping at *Signorelli's* for a coconut flat white, Maryam thought back to when she had just returned home from university all those years ago. She thought back to when she had first met Ava and Sofia. Back then, she had felt a loss of the life she had — she thought her formative years were over and she had returned to her many roles. A part of her then longed for the spontaneity of the life she had. A part of her wanted to be without consequence, without weight. She didn't anticipate what she had gained in that feeling of loss. It was Sofia who had, so beautifully, pointed it out.

"Maryam, take a step back." She had said. "Have you ever thought that maybe this — us — our friendship — is the abundance in the loss you feel? That perhaps, this, is the manifestation of everything going right that you are seeking, maybe it is the love and approval you are seeking from God?"

Maryam carried those words. Their friendship, she had decided, was characterised by milestone bonding. It was the bonding that happened when kindred spirits meet at a point of crossroads for them all and carry each other through, milestone to milestone. It was this friendship that was life-affirming.

And so, they spoke in prayers, they navigated their friendship with full awareness that they were an answer to each other's prayers. Their bond increased them in gratitude, it showed them a lens of love and hope they had not seen before and so they prayed, for continuance, for strength, for this to remain an anchor of sorts, through loss of life and through new life, through responsibility and every milestone.

With each other, they could always have a glimpse of the life they prayed for.

Demons

Shana Jasani

She was just two steps away
from ending the game
but she promised she wouldn't
in case you still came

but you didn't show up
you didn't come save her
so she let herself go
she lost all her hope

her friends told her to be happier
because they told her
'happy is better'
but no matter how hard she tried
it didn't get easier

so she sat in the corner
and watched them all laughing
eyes sunken in
and faith ever fading

she tore herself apart
and cut into her skin
she can't race her demons
they always seem to win

she took the pill
and as her throat began to swell
her eyes rolled back
and at last, her demons fell.

On the Blob

Ulka Karandikar

Maris Taylor knows everything there is to know about being a woman. She *swears* when it happens blood squirts out your tits like ketchup. I put my palms on my chest and press down hard, stemming the imaginary flow of blood soaking through my P.E. top. What would Mum say? Already *sick to the back teeth* of my mountain of washing. And *don't even* get her started on Dad's badminton socks.

"You're a slaggy little liar, Maris Taylor!" Rupa says. She's already dressed and putting on her hockey boots. "It comes out your fanny. That's what my mum says. And she's a doctor." Rupa's always going on about her mum being a doctor. I try to tell her it's boastful. But she just scoffs and goes back to doing it anyway. Non-stop.

"My Dad says your Mum's a dirty Paki." Maris says this with real venom and starts to put on her hockey boots, although she's not even got her top on yet. It's always a race between those two. I mostly stay out of it. Best not to get involved. Instead, I take out my damp socks and sit on the slatted bench.

Rupa calls Maris a racist bitch, whilst grabbing her scrunchie and trying to pull it off.

Maris retaliates by pinching Rupa's arm, "I'm gonna tell Miss Reilly if you don't pack it in, Rupa!"

They're my best friends.

My hockey socks smell like the back of Dad's shed. They've stayed in my locker for far too long. I unbunch the damp fabric and pull them over my hairy legs. I wish I was allowed to shave. I tried Dad's razor last month. Gashes marked my skin and oozed like sliced-open strawberry ice pops. It went everywhere. I managed to dump the bloodied bath mat next-door. Luckily, Rupa's Mum puts the bins out early for collection. Mum says she's a *bit like that*. Then I snuck back inside, just in time for our dinner bell. It's a porcelain Flamenco lady with a bell as a skirt and a frilly top. Dad got her on holiday before I was born. He says she's got musical lady-parts. Mum always tells him to *stop being so vulgar* in front of his daughter, and then lets him pat her on the bum. This happens every dinnertime. I wish they'd stop.

Rupa begins to scream. Maris lets go of her arm.

"How long does it last?" I ask Maris.

"What's that, Titch?" My nickname. Dad says all good things come in small packages, but I haven't managed to convince the class yet. I suppose I am short and maybe I do look like an Ewok.

"The *bleeding*. How long?" I'm desperate to know. This was bigger than Rupa and Maris's constant bickering. I wish they'd pack it in. Maris looks as if I've just told her Nick Owen's announced the death of her Mum on Central News. I can tell she's a bit put out by my questioning her.

She pauses and then offers, "Forever?"

Rupa scoffs, but I can tell she's just as worried as I am by this new bit of information. There's no talk about her doctoring mum now. "Really? Forever?" She asks quietly.

"Yeah...forever." Maris isn't used to Rupa's undivided attention. "I'm pretty certain...I guess." Maris chews the end of her ponytail. Her hair is shiny and always smells of her big sister's Dewberry body spray. Maris sprays it on her hair, on her fanny and under her arms. She says that's what Sandrine, her French pen pal, does. It's a bit too much, if you ask me, but of course — nobody ever does.

I want to know about the blood, "Is it like, all the time? Every day? Non-stop. Even when you're out in town with your Mum, or on the 51 bus?" I ask, panicking a little.

"No. Not every day stupid. You're such a baby, Titch. My sister has it every month. She's meaner. Tells me to get out of her room or she'll slap my gob to Pelsall."

"But don't the sheets get dirty?" I'm embarrassed by how much I care about the clean up. And I *do* care about it — quite a lot, actually — I can't rely on Rupa's Mum being obsessed with bin collection every month.

"Stop going on about the blood, Titch! My sister's got these pads. She wears them in her bra." Maris is more confident as she remembers the practicalities. I'm relieved.

"Oh right. Yeah. I've heard of them." Rupa says, armed crossed.

I haven't. But vaguely remember an advert on telly with a woman on roller-skates, having the time of her life with two Labradors. I wish I was allowed a dog. "But is there any way to stop it completely? Any way at all? It just sounds so...so — *messy.*"

Rupa and I are silent. We are waiting for Maris' answer.

Miss Reilly calls, "If the three of you girls aren't out here in EXACTLY ten seconds flat — so help me God and the sweet baby Jesus — I'll put you all in detention for the rest of your wilful little lives! Girls! Do you hear me?"

"Yes, Miss Reilly. Sorry Miss Reilly." Rupa says in her most Catholic voice; her eyes are fixed on Maris. She's still waiting. We both are. My left hockey boot hovers above my foot, laces dangling across the damp sock. The old pipes begin to gurgle. Outside, we hear the hiss of hydraulic doors opening, as the boys' school coach pulls up. Wednesdays is football. Fridays is cross-country, but we've got Maths on Fridays, so we never get to see them because we're stuck in class.

"So?" Rupa encourages Maris, "I mean you can't bleed forever...right? I mean that's not fair. Is it? Something must stop it." It didn't seem fair. No. And what about showering after PE? That bothered me too. When my boobs start to bleed, how am I supposed to cover them up as well as all the other things wrong with me: hairy legs, fat knees, hairy arms.

"Err. Well...yeah, it's not fair..." Maris says. It's as if she's hearing herself properly for the first time. She sounds uncertain. This makes me nervous — Maris Taylor is never uncertain. She'll set us straight in a minute. I wait. After all, she's seen Mark O'Connell's knob *and* she wears a bra. Maris Taylor knows everything there is to know about being a woman.

And then it happens. The unimaginable.

"Maybe... it *does* come out your fanny. Maybe, your mum's right, Rupa...after all." Maris Taylor — the most sophisticated girl in St Hilda's — has just admitted she might be wrong.

Rupa gets up, "You're full of shit Maris Taylor," she says, I can tell she's freaking out. "I'm gonna tell your mum the next time I come round to play. I'm tired of this. Titch, come on. Get my hockey stick. I've got some balls to hit." She leaves.

I start to follow Rupa, carrying both our hockey sticks, and my left boot, whilst hobbling along on one damp sock. I give Maris a little shrug. It's meant to say — sorry about today's changing room banter. Wasn't great, was it? Nothing personal. We'll do better next time.

But Maris doesn't look up.

Instead, she continues to stare at the gap between her legs whilst chewing the back of her thumb. She looks small against the high cast iron hooks and the jumble of all our school uniforms.

"Titch! Come on!" Rupa shouts. Miss Reilly blows the whistle for the game to start.

"Coming!" I yell. Suddenly afraid of being left alone with Maris Taylor and her silenced gob.

Dadi Maa and I Enter the Buffyverse

Karishma Sangtani

'Sunnydale: come for the food, stay for the dismemberment.'
– Xander, Buffy the Vampire Slayer

When I take dadi maa to Sunnydale, she dons a cream kurta
and loafers. She says the pointed tree by the high school
is a hand on God's clock. I say, maybe. And also,
this is where the mayor morphs into a snake demon.
His body one long lashing pipe. Crescent moons for teeth.

Dadi maa wafts up to a porch across the street, undisturbed
by the onset of ominous music. With her grey moustache
at the knocker, she tells me all the houses look the same.
I tell her, everything happens here. Resurrections go wrong,
re-ensoulments go better. Spike becomes somewhat loveable.

And only under this cloudless sky does my tongue pivot
to Sindhi. I say 'crescent'. I drop 'morphs'. I think 'vampire slayer!'
and the translation puffs into my mouth like a popcorn kernel.
As I let these buttery mounds slip out, dadi maa nods along.
    Her chin
a spade, scooping up syllables neither of us knew I could deliver.

The Trousseau

Samina H.Bakhsh

The trousseau was almost full. Just a few more items, thought Parveen, as she picked up a baby pink salwar kameez suit off the bed. She ran her weathered coarse fingertips along the delicate silver thread embroidery with pearl embellishments that outlined the heart shaped neckline, the cuffs of the sleeves and hem of the dress. A ray of sunlight peeking through the curtains caused the embroidery to sparkle. Parveen sighed. She gently removed the suit from its hanger, separating the top, trousers, and the chiffon dupatta before folding each piece, slowly and carefully. Stacking the items one on top of the other, she lowered them into the bridal chest, atop the dozens of other expensive traditional outfits, jewellery, and other special items a mother gifts her daughter before she embarks on her new life, just as her mother had done for her, and her mother's mother before that.

She smiled to herself. What would her friends and family say if they saw her? Parveen was not known for deliberating over simple tasks like this. No, Parveen worked fast. Just as her mother had taught her. Multi-tasking Queen they called her. Whether it was taking her youngest to his clubs, whilst listening to his Quran recitation and using the hands-free to place a grocery order. While cooking, checking homework, and folding the laundry in between. Or shopping, listening to her favourite qawwali, but also having a catchup with her sister on WhatsApp who was in a different time zone. Parveen liked to make the most of her time. Time wasn't to waste, as her mother had taught her, and her mother's mother before that. A good wife and a good mother always kept busy. It didn't really matter if she couldn't quite remember which colour belt her son had moved up to, or what exactly it was she had been texting her sister about. Parveen had learnt not to worry about that too much. Afterall everyone forgets things.

The trousseau was almost full, just one final gift to add for her daughter. Just as her own mother had done for her and her mother's mother before that. Parveen slowly got up and closed the lid on the wooden chest, pausing to admire the intricate hand carvings that covered it. She made her way downstairs, passing by the flower vines that adorned the banister, their pink and cream tones in keeping with the wedding theme. As she entered the kitchen, she could hear the melody of upbeat Pakistani wedding folk songs playing in the garden mingled with laughter and singing from family and friends who had started arriving a few days ago.

Instinctively she walked over to the cooker. Leaning down she pulled open the oven door and took out the steel tawa, familiar with its heavy weight and knowing to brace her wrist just enough to not cause a strain. The wooden handle had smoothened over the years, so she could no longer tell where her mother's fingerprints would've once been. A lump formed in her throat, catching her by surprise and she quickly brushed away the moisture gathering in the corner of her eye. From the drawer she pulled out one of the brightly coloured cloths used to wrap chapattis and unfolded it. It was a red and white paisley design. It suddenly occurred to her that the tawa had been wrapped in a red and white cloth when it had made its first journey to England with her all those years ago, a new bride, travelling to be with her new husband in a new world.

"A good wife will keep her husband and her family with this!" Her mother had told her the day before she was to leave. She carefully placed the tawa in the centre of the cloth and began folding in the corners.

"By beating them with it?" her younger sister had quipped at the time, giggling, as she made a not-so-subtle joke about how their mother would make empty threats to use it on them when they wouldn't listen. But their mother's stern look, had her quickly pretending to be busy with the ends of her braid to avoid catching their mother's eye.

Parveen gave a soft chuckle. She remembered it so well.

Her mother had been right. By the time they had arrived at the house she would call home for the first ten years of her new life in England, it was late. Her husband and his cousin had taken turns to drive the several hours drive from Heathrow to their small Northern town. Everyone was hungry. Parveen had inaugurated her arrival by unwrapping the tawa and preparing fresh chapattis for them all. Her husband and his cousin had insisted there was no need, they could get fish and chips, but she had no idea what that was. In fact, she didn't know or have any understanding of anything around her. Apart from the tawa her mother had told her to keep with her on the plane, lest it got damaged from being thrown around in the luggage hold.

Parveen remembered how her young handsome husband had beamed at her as he devoured home cooked chapattis for the first time in years. He had loved her spicy potato and onion paranthas made with desi ghee. He never asked for them, never wanting to make extra demands of her. But she knew, so she would have two piping hot and

34

ready for him once he'd return from his shift at the factory. The rich aroma filling the house, embracing him as he entered.

A tear rolled down her cheek as she recalled the memories. She had not used the tawa to make his favourite spicy potato and onion paranthas for many years now. The particular aroma was never to enter her home again.

Parveen finished wrapping up the tawa, tying opposite corners of the square cloth together, just as she had watched her mother do that night. She lifted the tawa and held it towards her chest and closed her eyes. She remembered she had held it just like this all the way until they had finally settled into their seats on the plane and the air stewardess had placed it in the overhead compartment. She hadn't liked it when she did that. It was the first thing she grabbed once they had been allowed to start taking their things down.

Moving to the kitchen table, Parveen sat down, bringing the wrapped tawa with her. She ran her hand over the cloth, tracing a finger along the paisley design. She had bought a new modern non-stick lightweight one from the local desi store, but her daughter had not been pleased at all upon seeing it.

"Why have you bought me this Ammi?" she had asked.

"Beta, it's a new fashion one," Parveen had explained. She was worried she had disappointed her daughter with her choice.

"But Ammi, I thought you were going to give me the tawa... y'know, like Naniji did for you, and Buri Nani did for her before that..." Her daughter had taken Parveen's hand in hers. Parveen had pulled her hand back, conscious that her fingers would scratch her daughter's delicate skin.

"Beta, what are you going to do with that useless old thing!" she had said, trying to laugh.

Suddenly Parveen stood up. With a quickness that was more her nature, she undid the two ties, leaving the chapatti cloth on the table as she made her way back to the cooker. The familiar clang of the tawa steel meeting the gas cooker top was soothing to her ears. Parveen clicked and turned the gas hob on and allowed the tawa to warm up, like it had done thousands of times already.

Whipping around to the fridge, she took out the Tupperware with the chapatti dough, placed it on the countertop and proceeded to take out the rolling pin and dish with chapatti flour she kept in the top drawer right next to the cooker. Flour to the left, dough to the right, pin in front of her. In a rhythm that was as familiar to her as her own heartbeat, Parveen scooped a portion of the dough, dipped in the flour and with repeated rolling and turning motions, she created perfect spheres. Parveen repeated this a few more times, knowing instinctively each was the same size as the one before, and the one after.

She then picked up each dough ball one at a time, a gentle tap to squash it down and then with both hands she rotated the edges of the dough ball between her fingers, flattening them out. Placed the flattened ball on the countertop and began to roll. The trick was to apply ever so slightly more pressure to one side of the chapatti as you rolled it, causing it to rotate, ending in a perfectly circular shaped chapatti. She gave a satisfied sigh as she placed the final one in the chapatti changear.

Parveen remembered when she had first started teaching her daughter.

"Beta, not like that, look at my hands and fingers, ok?" She had patiently explained to her young daughter.

"I can't do it, Ammi! And you're moving your hands too quickly, I can't even tell what you're doing!" Her daughter had cried out, as she dumped the peculiar shaped pile of dough on the counter.

Several weeks which turned to months had passed, but eventually one summer, her daughter proudly presented her father and her with several perfectly round chapattis. It was on this day that her beautiful daughter turned to her and said, "Ammi, I want this tawa when I get married!"

At the time, Parveen and her husband had laughed, but Parveen remembered how he had then taken her hand into his and given it a gentle squeeze. When she had turned to look his way, he was misty-eyed as he watched their daughter joyfully serve them her perfect chapattis. Parveen had smiled at him, but it hadn't quite reached her eyes. She filled her lungs with as much air as she could and slowly let it out.

A kaleidoscope of memories raced through her mind. The untouched roti by her husband's hospital bedside. Her middle son, arriving home from football, muddied head to toe every Saturday morning and calling out for breakfast paranthas. Or her youngest son and daughter who insisted that toast made on the tawa tasted infinitely better than from the toaster. They would only have it this way with their eggs. Or how her eldest daughter, battling a cold, would only eat chicken yukni with roti dipped in. The neighbourhood ladies who knew they could rely on Parveen Api to prepare a stack of over fifty chapattis effortlessly for all occasions.

Parveen took a deep sigh and swallowed the lump forming in her throat. Her tawa had served her well. It had kept the love flowing, had kept the bond growing between her husband and her, with her children, with her community. Her mother had been right. And now the time had come. Just as her mother had done for her, and her mother's mother before that.

"Ammi, are you ok?" Her daughter's voice suddenly broke her thoughts.

"Han, beta, I've made roti for everyone." Parveen quickly wiped another tear and went over to her daughter, embracing her.

Aisha lifted her arms laced with henna, high over her mother's shoulders and hugged her back.

"Ammi, you haven't packed the tawa away yet have you? I wanted to steam my mehndi over it, the lady said it helps with the colour."

"No, beta, it's still here, let me get the cloves, I'll pack it after that," Parveen said smiling. She kissed her daughter on the cheek, turned to light the fire under the tawa one last time, just like her mother did for her and her mother's mother before that.

Hijab Diaries: A New light

Bushra Shaikh

Eyes full of night, I rub them to blur
the tightly covered vision
of her.

Before me stands a woman, before me stood more.
Delicate apprehensions galore.

Part of a clan! Of course not, sorry I say.
A group, a tribe perhaps.
The chosen path for humans made by clay.

Islam, my love, all praise God got.
Begin this properly
let them not think façade,
of what?

A smile, the teeth gleaming white.
From the divine essence,
the presence,
of this new found light.

Noor, noor!
Light upon light.
A verse, that reminder again?
Maybe it's too early for...

Bright eyes now full of dawn,
different from the night before.
A Modesty would take shape today,
a new me, as I rub them sore.

Across This New Divide

Sara Summun Khan

'Take me home' says my grandmother. We are home but she doesn't recognise it. Her house has been remodelled to make things more comfortable for her. The foundations are the same, but the walls have been changed.

Ten years ago, my grandmother started to lose her memory. It started with the little things and developed into forgetting names and faces, towards the end it was everything except for prayer and some memories which she held onto. She remembers five times a day that her Lord calls her, and she will respond to His call, but will forget that she has broken half the bones in her body and will rise only to fall again, injuring herself beyond repair.

Her body is weak and as I hold her hand in mine, I look into her big beautiful eyes, which now have a glazed look to them. I see her defined nose and her ghostly white plait peeping out from under her scarf.

My grandmother, Sughra, wasn't always like this. As I gaze into her eyes, I wonder what she's thinking as I reassure her that I will take her home, knowing that she will ask me again in another ten minutes. I can feel her soul, so strong, wanting to run like the wind but inhibited by its weak shell.

People tell me my grandmother's stories before she arrives in the room. I am often curious about things I stumble upon in the house, such as the old hookah which stands in the corner of the new living room. In a time where women seldom smoked, Sughra, whose husband lived abroad, smoked this hookah under the guise to let thieves know that there was indeed a man in the house and its smoke danced around the cobbled streets keeping strangers at bay.

In a time when the country was one, Muslims, Hindus and Sikhs living together as neighbours and friends, looking after each other like brothers and sisters and forming bonds of friendship which went past differences.

Sughra lived in a small cobbled street in which there were only two houses. The other house belonged to a Hindu family who had been living there for a long time. Before my grandfather migrated to Kenya for work, my grandmother cared for their 5 young children. And long before local farmers struck Mughal gold in the dry summer soil, this was an uneventful village.

For many years, the neighbours lived side by side in peace and harmony, supporting each other in times of happiness and sorrow. However, a feeling of unrest was rippling through the nation affecting those who tried their hardest to claim ignorance. One could not close their eyes and ears from the news of new borders being drawn across the land and it was becoming hard not to notice one's differences.

After much rapid change in the country Sughra watched with a heavy heart as her neighbours packed up their belongings ready for their journey. They could only take as much as they could carry and with rumours of a troubled and violent journey ahead, they had to be very careful. After a few hours there was a knock on Sughra's door which she opened to a tearful face.

"My sister, the time has come," said her neighbour. In her hands, she held an old box.

"Is there anything I can do to make this easier?" my grandmother asked. Her neighbour held out the old box.

"Can I leave this in your care? As you know we do not have much money, within this box is all of my mother's gold, my beautiful bangles, my wedding necklace and a few small trinkets. They are not worth much, but they mean everything to me. Once we are settled in our new home, I pray I will be able to come back and collect my treasure."

Sughra took the box and prayed that her neighbours would return and that they would laugh together once again.

Years passed and Sughra's responsibilities increased. With a growing family, she had to divide her time between her children and looking after her community as the aftermath of partition affected them all. It was hard to accept that the people with whom they had shared hookahs had to leave everything; their schools, their businesses, and their friends. Sughra often thought about her neighbour, where had she settled, if she was happy and if she would ever return?

The summers of the Punjab had always been long and hot but every now and then there was a change in atmosphere. A cool wind would arrive and dance around everyone's sticky limbs and the smell of soil would hit your nostrils. It was a promise of rain. The droplets of heaven were so beautiful and people would stand outside waiting for it to hit their foreheads and cool their souls.

Sughra sat in her chair on the veranda waiting for the rain and as the first drops hit the floor there was a loud knock on her door. As she crossed the veranda the rain became heavier. The guest at the door was almost unrecognisable but when the person spoke Sughra recognised the soft voice. "Sister, it is me," spoke her neighbour.

Hours later after the tears were shed and the tea cups empty, my grandmother looked at her companion carefully, she had lost weight and aged, however a smile rested on her face.

The two women shared stories of family, health, politics and eventually the conversation steered to wealth.

"Are you comfortable sister?" Sughra asked in a concerned voice.

She was one of the few women in the village whose husband worked abroad and sent her money to keep afloat and distribute to others in need. Her neighbour spoke to her of her struggle. Like so many others, they had next to nothing when they reached their final destination. They had used their skills to start businesses and form communities.

My grandmother's neighbour looked at her feet shyly and asked after her old box. She did not expect my Sughra to still have it, after all everyone had felt the repercussions of partition.

"I hid the box in a safe place for a long time," replied Sughra. She thought back and sighed.

Her neighbour took this as a sign that her box had been lost, misplaced or even sold.

There was no further talk on the matter, it had been a while since the box had been given to Sughra's care and despite her trust in my grandmother, her neighbour had been sceptical given the political climate at the time.

People had been turned against one another. Sughra's neighbour had to choose leaving the box behind or to risk becoming the target of looters along the way. She had chosen the former knowing full well her Muslim neighbour could do what she wanted with it as she may never have been able to return to it.

Sughra prepared a bed for her weary guest. She knew her old neighbour had thought that she may have sold the contents of the box, but in fact she had not. She had held her neighbour's treasure close to her heart all those years with the hope that its owner would return. Just as Sughra knew she would return to her Creator one day.

She had hidden the box to avoid suspicion from local thieves under an area of loose flooring in the very same room its owner was now in. If her instincts were right, the owner's curious nature would lead her to find her treasure tonight.

As her neighbour tried to sleep, she could not stop thinking of her possessions. She wandered over to the kitchen, opened and closed cupboards and then went into the living room to try and spot any hidden corners but after a while of searching, she stopped. What was she doing?

She was exhausted, it had been a long journey back to Pakistan. She went back to her room and tripped over the rug. As she bent down to straighten it, she lifted a corner and realised the purpose of the fabric. It seemed to be concealing an uneven floor. Lifting the rug she could see a whole slate had not been sealed properly. She lifted the slate and the contents beneath made her gasp.

Under these floorboards Sughra had saved books. Dozens of books. Books on religion, books on politics and poetry. To anyone else who would stumble upon this secret collection, they would see no value in the books. But upon closer inspection, each book contained money. Coins had been wrapped in paper and had been concealed within covers and notes stuffed discreetly within pages. Amongst these books was a dusty old box. Sughra's neighbour picked up her box and started to cry. She could not believe she was seeing her possessions after so long.

She wiped away the tears and fell asleep cradling generations of gold in her arms as if it were a child.

The next morning Sughra prepared breakfast and waited for her companion who appeared shyly holding her weathered box.

She sat down. "I cannot thank you enough, our country has been divided due to our differences. But I have learnt today that it is our humanity that binds us together. You have always been generous but today I have seen how big your heart is. Power has led our nations to ruin, it has made us forget the good in ourselves and others. This divide has put fear into the hearts of people. That being different makes you dangerous, when it is the opposite. It is these differences that encourage us to reach out to one another and realise we need one another."

After sharing the meal accompanied with old memories the two women embraced. One set off on her long journey home while the other continued hers.

After her neighbour left, Sughra sat down in her favourite chair and looked at her husband's recent letter. She missed him and wanted to share this story with him. She began writing her response detailing everything that had happened and how their old neighbour had returned. It would take over three months before her husband would read her story and reply but she would wait patiently just like she had always done.

Over the years my grandmother has told me this story again and again. And I wonder how she could recall these stories but not recall my name, her own children and home?

My grandmother nudges me, 'I'd really like to go home now,' she says again in a childish manner.

I catch my breath and feel guilty. I can feel the beautiful nostalgia while she cannot.

"I'll take you,' I say. I carry her weak frame from one room to another. She falls asleep and I know when she wakes up she will be content for ten minutes until she asks me again.

Alzheimer's took over my grandmother's brain and old age her soul and body. She deteriorated quickly and all the stories vanished from her mind, slipping from her fingers as she tried to catch them just like the cool summer breeze before the rainfall.

My grandmother passed away on the same day as Pakistan experienced one of its most powerful earthquakes. My family's heart broke into small pieces just like the rubble of the buildings that had fallen to the ground. We had lost a legend, a soul whose mind may have been erased, but her memory will always live on.

Synonyms For Paradise

Zara Sehar

And when we talk about paradise
part of me hopes my heaven on earth walks
long enough to illuminate life for me

with her own two hands she sits by the
heater and oils my hair
saying lambay bal hona chaihay and
to the rhythm of her voice, my hair grows and it shines
and it grows so long it sends whispers down my spine

and when we talk about paradise
I talk about my Mother
how heaven has more than a few homes and
one is beneath her
and in this case, it feels warm under feet that are a size 4

and when we talk about paradise
I talk about how heaven leaves footprints
In and out of the snow
carrying aromas from before I was born
heaven lays footprints everywhere I walk
on the same ground my forehead longs to know

and so, when we talk about paradise
I say mines always home
her name is universal
and her Jannah is the one I love to call home

Twelve Minutes Ago

Sairish Hussain

The father was slumped against the steering wheel, blood trickling down his nose. The baby wailed over the car alarm. The mother was in the backseat. Her head rested perfectly against a cracked window, a circle of shattered glass laced with blood, like a bullet hole targeted on her forehead. Smoke billowed from the car and the baby wailed with ferocity, almost as if the fumes were coming from the infant's lungs. This was not the plan as they left the hospital that morning. They cradled their new-born, anxious and protective, strapping her into the baby seat and ready to start the rest of their lives. The mother's body was not even close to being healed. Her stomach was tender, the C-section scar throbbing under the bandages. Overwhelmed with fatigue and pure bliss, she marvelled at the strength in her baby's fist, the way it gripped her finger tightly. The father kept throwing back loving glances, his eyes fixed on the rear-view mirror rather than on the road. Twelve minutes ago, life was just beginning.

If only the father had taken a different route. If only his car had failed to start. The blood would run back up his nose, his bones would pop back into place and the car would be speeding away from the wreckage. Metal and plastic, glass and dirt would assemble and fix themselves into their allotted positions. The red-haired man from the colliding car would not be lying face down in the middle of the road, limbs bent at odd angles, blood seeping from his head. He'd fly back inside the windscreen, the fragments of glass following him like a magnet. They would slot back in with ease, like the pieces of a jigsaw. The man would still be fuming about the argument with his wife. That was thirty-two minutes ago.

"*Bitch!*" he'd shouted, as he'd slammed the door shut. He worked so hard during the harshest of winters, digging up roads and laying down pipes in motorways. His face was weathered with biting winds, his hands calloused with heaving dirt, and all she ever did was nag him all the time. He revved the engine and growled before racing off down the road. He wouldn't be back for dinner tonight, he thought. Not knowing that he wouldn't be back forever.

This wasn't what either of them had planned, those broken people lying spreadeagled on the middle of a remote country lane. A queue formed behind them of early morning commuters, some rolling their eyes at the inconvenience. They had important meetings to get to. Those closest to the crash ran forward to help. Seventeen calls were made to the ambulance and fire engine crews. *We can't get the baby out!*

"How are they going to get through here?" they asked one another, eyes tracing the gridlocked, narrow country lane.

A woman was on her way to collect her father from the airport. He was flying in to attend her graduation ceremony the following day. Her eyes kept resting on the driver of the car parked behind her. He was handsome, the young man who had his dad and granddad in the seats next to him. They'd planned a road trip to the Lakes, an excuse to spend 'quality time'. Three generations in one car, imagine if they had been wiped out that morning.

"What if it blows up?" a child whispered to his mother who shushed him quickly. They were on the opposite side of the road, with a clear view of the red-haired man on the ground.

It was a morning filled with disrupted plans, least of all for the mother and father who had only parented for around 48 hours. They were going to wait on their baby hand and foot. To scoop her up from her cot if she let out a single sound, place a bottle in her mouth so hunger wasn't felt for more than a couple of minutes. But now the baby's wails were mixed with car alarms which rang out in unison. Sirens screamed in the distance. Vehicles moved with no room to spare to allow them to pass through.

Everyone would find out now. When the funerals were over and it was decided who would take care of the child, they would all find out. Family would search through their home and empty drawers, throw clothes into bin liners ready to be taken to the charity shop, the nursery would be dismantled. A life that almost was. Somebody would find the secret stash of money that the mother was hiding. It was wrapped tightly with a rubber band in a nook on her side of the wardrobe. There was an emergency suitcase in the garage too, the one packed with essentials for a quick getaway.

The mother's phone was not crushed in the wreckage. Those searching wouldn't even have to scroll through it to find text messages and phone calls from the other man. The good one, who promised to take her away from everything and be a father to the then, unborn child. The life that the mother dreamt of didn't include the man who was slumped over the steering wheel. It was a nice change to have him dripping blood, with torn ligaments and a bruised face. Twenty-two minutes ago, they'd left the maternity ward pretending to be a happy couple. The mother gripping their bundle of joy, who was still inside her stomach when the husband had punched and thrown her to the ground. It continued throughout the pregnancy, just like it had done throughout their marriage.

They would have a different life, the mother thought, caressing her newborn as they set off towards home. She would recover from the birth, wait for the child to settle into the world, and then meet her lover during one of her husband's work trips. She would disappear with her baby and the good man, who had waited patiently for her for years. They would have a different life, the mother thought, caressing her newborn as they set off towards home. But that was twelve minutes ago.

The red-haired man had come speeding around the corner doing 50mph on a 30mph road. Tears of anger blurred his vision as he relayed the latest argument with his wife. This time she accused him of lying about his whereabouts on a Saturday night two months ago. Last week it was cheating with one of his colleagues. The week before that, it was about not giving her enough money to pay the water bill. He'd started dreading going home, tip toeing around her outbursts, placating her with whatever she wanted to hear. Going grey rock. He should have gotten out years ago. Before she became consumed with anger and bitterness. Whenever he said that to her, her response was always the same.

"Six miscarriages. I had six miscarriages."

Now they would all find out. Once postmortems were carried out and he was six feet under, they would all find out. How he'd made a secret doctor's appointment after ignoring the symptoms for months. The blood in his stool, the pain in his abdomen, the unexplained loss of his weight. He'd had a long thin tube inserted into his anus last week. The small camera attached at the end had discovered a tumour in his bowel. There was no hand intertwined with his as the doctor told him he had cancer three days ago, no shoulder to cry on, no warm-filled embrace or words of comfort. Just images of death flooded his mind. *His* death. His unfulfilled, loveless life. And what his family and friends would say about him if he was to die.

That happened sooner rather than later and now he lay on the cold, icy concrete whilst paramedics covered his body and told the public to back away.

"We'll have to cut these two from the car," one firefighter said to another just as it started to rain. "And for God's sake get the baby out!"

When news reached the midwife that the infant had returned to the hospital alone, she gasped and said a prayer.

"Poor lady," she said, remembering the mother. Most women cried when they held their babies for the first time. This one shed tears from her heart and had held onto the infant for dear life.

"And what about the dad? He was such a gent."

The other midwives nodded their heads in agreement. "He was...he was," they agreed.

In a nearby GP surgery, a doctor scanned her list for the day. A black ring encircled the name of the patient who had an appointment at 10.30am.

"Deceased? How?"

"Car crash, yesterday," the assistant replied.

"Good grief... first he finds out he has cancer, then dies a few days later."

"Yeah, poor guy. And his poor wife."

The poor wife was prepared to grieve forever for her six unborn children, but not for the husband, who she thought would be around forever. She treated him dreadfully. She knew that. Partly because he didn't view the miscarriages as the losses that they were. They *were* children, as far as she was concerned, so why didn't he participate in her grief? Why didn't he participate in her rage?

When the poor wife heard about the cancer diagnosis, days after her husband's death, she wept. What must have been going through his mind? Guilt stabbed at her, but she couldn't help but feel relieved that he hadn't told her. How would she have coped? Maybe it was better this way. A shock to the system. She had enough pain to consume the two of them, enough hurt to carry them through until the end. Her friends, the 'career women', were now breastfeeding and buying baby-grows. Her sister, who became pregnant after a brief fling, was now a rebranded 'Instagram mum', using her baby as a prop to build a following. As they creeped into their thirties, all the women around her had changed. They were no longer Claire, Frances, or Anita. They were mothers. *Mothers.* And here she was, her womb aching, her home empty of cooing and giggling and the pitter patter of tiny feet. And now her husband was gone too.

The poor wife had heard of the orphaned baby. How she'd grieved for the mother. The poor wife imagined her packing up her newborn with the utmost care and heading for home. But the destination was snatched away from her. The wife wondered who would now be taking care of the baby. Would it be the grandparents, aunties and uncles?

It only took a few enquiries before she found out exactly where the child lived and who was looking after her. A stressed-out auntie had stepped in, a woman with two children of her own. The poor wife had seen her juggling prams and toddlers alongside her food shop whilst the miserable-looking husband drove off to work every day and escaped the hullabaloo. The poor wife often wondered whether she should go and help before dragging herself away and giving herself a telling off. She should not be there, watching from a distance.

Years later, as loneliness became her constant companion and stitched itself onto her shadow, the poor wife would think about the child. The auburn-haired girl would creep into her dreams, appear at the bedside in the middle of the night, arms outstretched, wanting to be held. If the six children she had lost had ever survived, they would look like the auburn-haired girl, a trait inherited from her dead husband.

Instead, the poor wife went from one bad date to the next. She met unremarkable men. Not so unlike her husband. It wasn't a man she wanted. It was the child.

She was at school now. She was always thrown out of the car by the miserable-looking husband. She'd go bounding into the building, full of enthusiasm. During playtimes, the girl was animated, a storyteller, and always surrounded by other kids. A popular little missy. The guardians were often late picking her up. The stressed-out auntie and the miserable-looking husband. Rushing around, panicking and shouting at her to jump into the car. The girl would become silent and subdued as she stepped in.

Not long after, the poor wife noticed something else. She was not alone. There was somebody else watching. A man who came almost as regularly as she did. When she followed his gaze, he was always watching the auburn-haired child. *Her* child. At first, the poor wife's heart filled with terror. Who was this man? Was he a predator? She thought to report him to the school but how would she explain who she was? A woman standing outside the school with no son or daughter to pick up and take home. Just like the man.

After that, she began to observe the man just as closely as she did the little girl. He said nothing. He did nothing. He just watched from afar and as soon as the child was out of sight, he would turn and walk away, with pain etched all over his face. The poor wife concluded: he was not a bad man. If anything, he was a good man. Someone connected to the child in some way. And he was hurting, just like she was.

The good man's visits decreased over time, but he never truly went away. Just as the poor wife thought that she would never see him again, he would reappear. She would spot him in the distance, smiling sadly at the little girl.

He was there on that day too. When she finally came face to face with him. The guardians were late again. Outrageously late. The teachers were getting frustrated, checking their watches and making phone calls. There were mutterings of taking the children back inside. They weren't paying attention; they were too busy moaning about hitting traffic and not making it home in time for tea.

The poor wife's legs started to carry her towards the child at the gates. Her auburn plaits were swinging, her little face emotionless as she squinted into the distance, waiting for the miserable-looking husband to pick her up.

The poor wife didn't care, time stood still and everyone around her disappeared. She was finally going to take her.

She would never be late; she would never make the girl wait. As she walked, the poor wife didn't notice the man who was walking towards her but from the opposite direction. The good man, whose dreams were snatched away from him. The dream was right before him now. She looked just like her mother, the woman he had loved and lost. He couldn't bear the thought of losing the child too, the only thing that connected him to his past. He had followed her for all these years. She was just within his reach. He didn't notice the woman walking in the same direction, the one who had desperate tears in her eyes. They were almost there, one more step and the child would be theirs.

They reached out and touched her at the same time.

May 11ᵗʰ 1985

Mariyam Karolia

He sees his pardesi
As he beholds the tiger-skin agni
Lighting up the afternoon
"Chai ba'now amreh!"

He leads you to the dival
Gives you time to catch your breath
As he lays our kamar across your shoulders.
The smallest gesture from one insan to another

In a moment of insanity.
More came to sit on the dival
Silent, for the survival of pandemonium
Takes the baraf from your veins.

And in this forgotten kona
A kinship of nuqsan and pain
Is forged in cups of PG Tips.
As they pass those lips,

That will never ask again
"Why don't you go home?"
He refuses your "thanks mate"
As he walks you to your car,

Makes sure you are safe to drive
But you shake his hand anyway.
He nods. "Ah cheh maru Bradford, maru City."
You smile. "Allez Bantams."

The Shape of a Girl

Dipika Mummery

Sachi had followed the girl with a soul full of spite. She returned shaking with fear and disgust, longing lapping at the edges of her thoughts.

The girl, Mina, had arrived in the village three moons ago. She was a distant young cousin of Hari, Sachi's great-aunt and the elder woman of the village – so distant that they did not even share the same skin colour. Hari, Sachi and the other villagers were the deep-baked shade of long days spent toiling in the salty heat of this part of the coast. Mina was pale, with pebble-smooth skin and eyes that glowed green like the sea in the height of summer. The men and children of the village still stared at her, while the women had long since decided to look away unless she addressed them directly, which she rarely did. When she did speak, her voice was petal-soft even as she tried to fit her wide, maroon lips around the village dialect with a clumsy grace. She brought her hands to her mouth often when speaking, and looked down shyly whenever anyone spoke to her, even if it was a woman, which made Sachi roll her eyes in impatience.

Sachi, one year older than the girl, noticed all of these qualities because she knew she did not possess them herself. All she had ever known was the village, its people and the sea with its capricious moods. There was nothing remarkable about her wiry dark hair, her deep brown eyes, her clumsy grace and the bitterly sharp edge to her voice, as her cousins often reminded her unkindly. Her bleed had started five moons ago. Instead of bringing a softness to her skinny chest and limbs, it had only gifted her with pimples and an oily sheen to her hair. Like the other villagers, she wore rough, well-worn tunics that lent themselves to the physical exertion of life on a remote coast, but did nothing for her appeal to men. Mina, however, seemed to have a new tunic for each moon.

When Mina had been in the village for one turning of the moon, Sachi noticed that she did not always stay until the end of the communal evening meal. The villagers came together at the end of each day to share whatever the fisherpeople and hunters had caught that day over twin fires in the village clearing. They ate briny fish and clams when the sun was high and the sea was warm enough to bathe in, and sea boar and algae when ice hung from the cliffs like fangs. When they had finished eating, the villagers would share stories. Some were retold over and over, the tales changing shape depending on who recounted them. Others sprung newly formed from the imaginations of both young and old. Some were gentle parables with a lesson to be learned. Others were so fantastic, so monstrous, that they made children cry and adults flinch at shadows for several nights afterwards.

All knew the carpenter Midnak to be the best storyteller. Each time, he would tell unfamiliar legends that he claimed were from the mountains or the forest on the other side of the world, flickering shadows from the dwindling fires dancing across his bearded face. Occasionally, the young goatherd Selmi would sing a song of the sea, her words and gently wavering voice so mournful that the villagers would wake the next day filled with an inexplicable sadness. Midnak and Selmi were gifted, the villagers believed, and so they honoured them accordingly with the first cup of autumn wine or thick, crumbling slabs of young pressed cheese. Sachi sometimes wondered if she would ever develop such a gift, unremarkable as she was. She hungered for something, anything, to elevate her from her life of few friends and eternal drudgery. Yet she never quite had the courage to take up the opportunity to change her circumstances, or to create it for herself. The unknown did not sit well in the community that had raised her despite the circumstances of her birth. She knew what happened to girls who forgot their place from the stories she heard about her own mother.

Sachi saw that Mina would sometimes quietly slip away after eating and listening to the stories and singing with intent eyes. She would bend to whisper quietly to Hari, then melt into the lengthening night.

Mina did this three times before Sachi decided to follow her. She knew that Mina did not immediately return to the hut she shared with Hari. Sachi always sat facing the huts, away from the darkening sea, during the evening meal. She never once saw the flicker of a lamp announce Mina's arrival through the slits in the hut's walls. So Mina went somewhere else, and without a lamp to light her way. A tryst, thought Sachi, scornfully, enviously, although she was puzzled by who the girl might be meeting. It seemed that all the men and boys of the village remained at the gathering each time Mina disappeared.

The fourth time, Sachi got up as soon as the girl had turned her back on the evening gathering, telling her mother that she was tired and wanted to go to sleep early. Midnak had just finished the tale of an ancient bird monster, bigger than a man, that once did battle with a wolf-like beast over a far-off territory on the other side of the restless sea. The villagers sat quietly before their voices rose in approval of the story, like a flock of raven wings spiralling skywards from the cliffs above.

When the hubbub died down, Sachi made her way towards her own hut, keeping Mina's soft footsteps within earshot, then abruptly changed direction when she heard Mina turn towards the path leading up to the cliffs above the beach. The waxing moon in the pristine night sky offered just enough light to see by, although Sachi knew the path, rock by rock, without having to see it. She remained several steps behind the girl, who toiled more slowly up the path. Not once did she turn around. Foolish girl, thought Sachi. Whatever Mina was up to, she would witness it and ensure she was punished by the elders. Sachi would prove that Mina's arrival was a change too far for their ancient community. The fact of her own mother's fall from grace – with a visiting sailor whose skin was as unnaturally pale as curdled milk, according to the stories – would no longer dog her every move. She would finally show that she was just as invested in keeping the village pure and free from evil as the elders who had banished her mother when Sachi was just a baby.

Mina reached the clifftop and walked to the very edge. Sachi crouched behind a rocky outcrop just a few steps away with her breath held like a great secret inside her. Mina stood as still as a hunted sand boar, moments before its death.. She looked up at the moon and stretched out her arms. Sachi held her breath. The girl looked as if she was about to fall forward and smash every single one of her bones on the rocks below. The moon's cold, dim light intensified and danced along the tops of her arms and across her upturned face, making her look like a slender mountain with a snowy peak. Sachi's heart hammered inside her chest, her throat, her head, her stomach. Just as she was about to leap up and pull Mina back from the edge, the feathers appeared.

One by one, they burst through the girl's skin in a neat row from shoulder to hand on both arms. Although they ran maroon with blood, the feathers' iridescence split the moon's light into pirouetting shards of purple and silver, dazzling Sachi where she remained crouched behind the rock. More feathers materialised down the sides of the girl's legs. Sachi almost retched at the sight of the sturdy tips thrusting through the tender skin. Sourness filled her mouth and she struggled to remain silent. She did not want to attract the girl's — or whatever she was now — attention.

But Mina's eyes were still fixed on the moon, and her arms remained stretched towards it as large, pale spikes tore through her tunic to march down the length of her spine. She turned slightly. With a sharp, cold sense of horror, Sachi realised that the girl's face had started to change shape, casting off the glow of the moon as fur sprouted across her brow and down her elongating face. The feathers on her body had grown and now hung from her limbs, swinging in the night sea breeze.

The shock of recognition was as sharp as a needle pressed into Sachi's palm. "Story eater," she mouthed to herself, her eyes wide and her arms and neck prickling.

The transformation must have been complete, for the girl — the beast? — spread her arms wider and leaned forward slightly. Sachi put her hand to her mouth in an unthinking imitation of Mina's own gestures of modesty — gestures that Sachi had once scorned her for.

The girl-beast bent her feathered legs, then sprang upwards. She seemed to hang in the air for one long interminable moment, then her arms moved up and down and she suddenly became not a girl with wings, but a bird-beast in the shape of a girl. Sachi's legs cramped. She stood up, thinking it safe to do so now that the beast was flapping its wings to take itself away from the edge of the cliff. The movement caught one of those sea-green eyes and it turned in the air, arms beating quickly, and stared at Sachi for a moment before rotating again and soaring up, up, away into the embrace of the moon. Sachi shuddered and retched again, finally emptying her stomach of its contents. She would never forget that wolfish face with the girlish eyes, not for as long as she lived. She looked up again and searched the sky for a glint of purple and silver wings.

She saw only the limitless night stretching over the dark sea.

The Word

Zaffar Kunial

I couldn't tell you now what possessed me
to shut summer out and stay in my room.
Or at least attempt to. In bed mostly.
It's my dad, standing in the door frame
not entering — but pausing to shape advice
that keeps coming back. "Whatever is matter,

must *enjoy the life.*" He pronounced this twice.
And me, I heard wrongness in putting a *the*

before *life.* In two minds. Ashamed. Aware.
That I knew better, though was stuck inside
when the sun was out. That I'm native here.
In a halfway house. Like that sticking word.
That definite article, half right, half
wrong, still present between *enjoy* and *life.*